BONJOUR, LONNIE

Faith Ringgold

HYPERION BOOKS FOR CHILDREN
NEW YORK

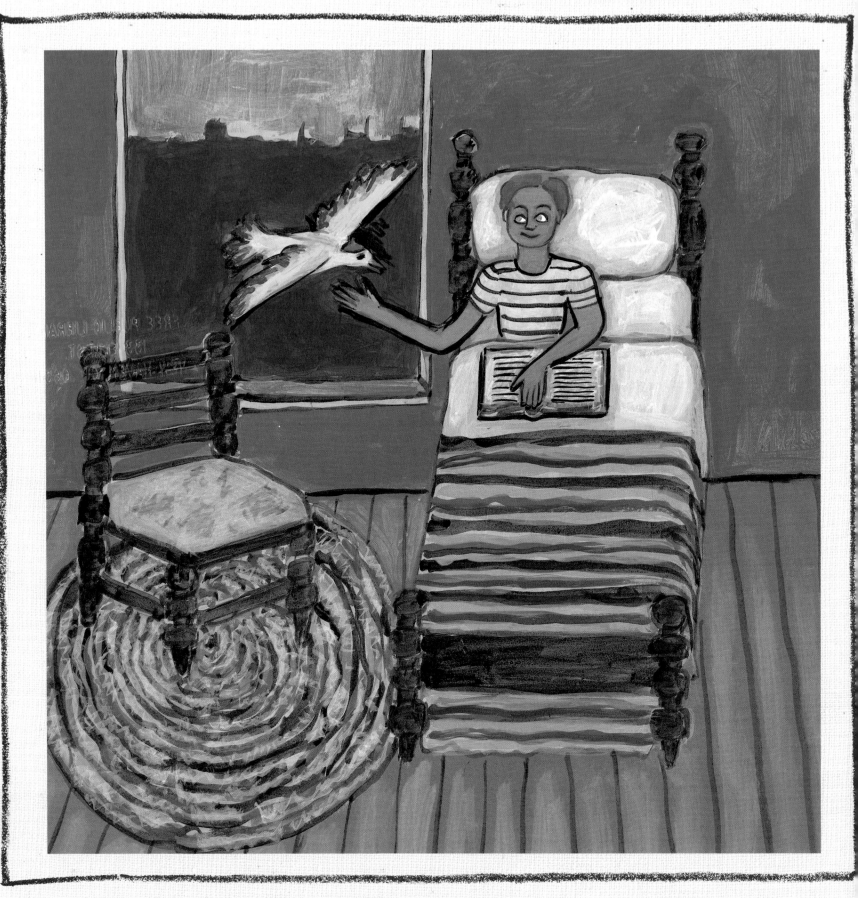

An extraordinary thing happened one night. It began with the song of a bird. I heard the singing and before I could open the window, the bird flew right in and perched on my finger.

"*Bonjour, Lonnie. Je m'appelle l'Oiseau d'Amour*," said the beautiful bird. "My name is Love Bird."

"Are you truly real, Love Bird," I asked, "or are you magic?"

"I am real, Lonnie, though in Paris they say I am magic because wherever I am people find their loved ones."

"I am an orphan, Love Bird. Can you find my loved ones?" I asked.

"*Au revoir, Lonnie*," was all Love Bird said, and he flew out my window.

"Come back, come back, Love Bird," I yelled. "I want you to be my friend." But the beautiful Love Bird was gone.

I pressed my face to the windowpane, hoping to see the beautiful Love Bird, but the street was changed. I ran outside to discover I was in the city of Paris. The people were dressed in old-fashioned clothes and they spoke French, just like Love Bird.

"*Bonjour, Lonnie*," they greeted me.

"*Bonjour, madame. Bonjour, monsieur*," I responded. "Have you seen Love Bird?"

"*Oui*," they said. "If you look everywhere you will find him."

I hurried to *la cathédrale de Notre-Dame de Paris*. I ran up the old winding stairs to the bell towers to ask the griffins and gargoyles if they had seen Love Bird.

"You must keep looking, Lonnie. Love Bird is everywhere," they told me.

I climbed to the top of *la Tour Eiffel*, which overlooks all of Paris.
"Love Bird! Love Bird!" I called out. "Where are you?"
But the beautiful Love Bird did not answer me.

I went to *le museé du Louvre* to ask the *Mona Lisa*
if she had seen Love Bird.
"I am looking for Love Bird, too," said the great painting.
"He makes me smile."

I marched up the *Champs-Elysées* and stood under the *Arc de Triomphe*. "*Vive la France! Vive la France!*" everyone yelled as they passed by. "Have you found Love Bird?"

"No," I said, "and I have searched all of Paris!"

"Do not give up," they yelled back. "Love Bird *is* Paris."

I ran to the river *Seine*. I crossed from *la rive droite* to *la rive gauche*—from the Right Bank to the Left Bank—stopping to ask the artists and the antique book sellers on the *quai*. I walked till my legs were so heavy I could not move them. "Love Bird," I cried as loudly as I could. "Please find me! I am lost!"

At that moment Love Bird appeared and perched on my finger.

"*Bonjour, Lonnie.* You are not lost. *Suis-moi,* follow me, and you will find your loved ones," said the beautiful Love Bird.

Speechless, I followed Love Bird into a courtyard. And once again he flew through a window and was gone.

The window opened and an old man called out to me: "*Lonnie, Lonnie!
Viens!* Come here. I am your grandpa. Your grandma and I have been waiting
for you."

"*Où étais-tu?* Where have you been?" asked Grandma.

"I have been looking for Love Bird," I answered.

"And you have found us," said Grandma.

"Come in, Lonnie," Grandpa said. "We know you have been wondering about
your family and what happened to your mother and father."

"Please tell me, Grandpa," I said. "I want to know why I don't have parents like other children, and why are you black and Grandma white?"

"Lonnie, I grew up a poor boy in Harlem. I sang in the church choir and dreamed of going to Europe to study opera."

"Oh, Grandpa, singing opera is my dream, too," I said excitedly.

"Your father had a beautiful voice also," said Grandma.

"When World War I began," Grandpa continued, "I joined the 369th Infantry and was sent to Champagne, a wine-growing province east of Paris. The French people there were friendly, hardworking, everyday folks. We learned to speak French and to love French food, which was not too different from the down-home dishes we had been raised on.

"I sang with the 369th Regiment band," said Grandpa.

"And I came to hear the music," said Grandma. "You may not believe this but I could cut a mean rug, Lonnie. The French people loved the music. They called it *le Jazz Hot*."

"Nowhere had I ever felt so at home outside the company of my family and friends. I fell in love with France forever," said Grandpa.

"And I fell in love with your grandpa," Grandma said. "He was so tall and handsome in his army uniform, and he was a hero, too."

"The French called us the Harlem Hell Fighters. We were the first Americans to win the *Croix de Guerre*, one of France's highest medals of honor. When the war was over we paraded down Fifth Avenue in New York City as heroes. The street was lined with cheering crowds. Confetti fell from the windows like snow. For the first time I felt respected, jubilant, victorious, and proud," said Grandpa.

"It was just fifty-five years after emancipation, and black people in America had a new sense of pride," Grandpa went on. "In Harlem, an exciting movement was born—we called it the Harlem Renaissance. It was there that Marcus Garvey started the Back to Africa Movement and Josephine Baker sang and danced at the Cotton Club. Our famous African American writers wrote novels and poems that made black writers accepted all over the literary world," said Grandpa.

"And the artists painted pictures of beautiful black faces for the first time," said Grandma.

"But still there was very little opportunity for a creative black person to achieve success in America," Grandpa told me. "In some places, we still could not eat at a lunch counter or drink from a public water fountain or reserve a hotel room. I longed to return to France, to feel free.

"So I went back to Paris. Paris was the place to go after the war," said Grandpa. "Many black Americans were living there. We met in the cafés and talked and talked about our hopes and dreams. My hope was to become an opera singer and to marry the lady I loved—your grandma."

"Oh, yes," said Grandma, "we had wonderful dinner parties for the artists and writers in our old Paris flat. Your grandpa became a famous singer not only in Paris but also in opera houses in Berlin and Vienna. After dinner he would entertain us with his beautiful tenor voice.

"Your father was just a baby then, Lonnie."

Just then the scene changed like in a movie, and Grandma and Grandpa were joined by new people seated around the table.

"I know who you are!" I said with joy. "You are my mother," I said to the lady with the green eyes. "And you are my father," I said to the man in the army uniform. "And the baby sitting on my grandma's lap is me! There is so much I want to know! Father," I said, "please tell me all about your life."

"My name is Lonnie Sr., my son," Father said. "And you look just like me, only you have your grandma's red hair and your mother Claudine's green eyes. I was a promising student of voice, only nineteen years old when I lost my life fighting for France in World War II."

"But why did you have to go to war and die for France, Father?" I asked.

"There was a man named Hitler who believed that the German people were a master race and that all Jews should be exterminated. You see, Lonnie, though we were both French, I was a black man but your mother was a Jew."

I wanted to hear from my mother, Claudine. "Why did you leave me, Mother?" I asked.

"Lonnie, my darling," Mother said, "you were such a good boy, no mother could have asked for a sweeter baby. But when the Nazis took over Paris, I feared for your safety. I had no choice but to give you away—"

"Whom did you give me to, Mother?" I interrupted.

"Her name was Clara Lee. She was an African American student studying at the Sorbonne in Paris. All Americans had to leave Paris, so I asked Clara Lee to take you to America with her," said Mother.

"But what happened to you, Mother?" I asked.
"I tried to hide, Lonnie, but the Nazis found me," said Mother sorrowfully,
"and took me away. Clara Lee will tell you the rest, my son."

"I smuggled you out of France with the help of the resistance movement," continued Clara Lee. "I hoped to make a home for you in America, but I became ill and couldn't take care of you. I wanted my aunt Connie and uncle Bates to take you, but I could not find them. So you were put in an orphanage," said Clara Lee.

"But now we have good news. Love Bird has found Aunt Connie and Uncle Bates," said Father. "They want to be your parents and give you a good home and the love you have missed."

"And Aunt Connie has dyed her own graying locks red like yours," said Mother. "They are waiting for you in the real world, my son."

"But I want to stay here forever with all of you," I said.

"Lonnie you must leave us," said Mother. "We are the past. We want you to have a future in the real world."

"*Au revoir, Lonnie*. We love you," they chorused. Once more the scene changed, and they were gone.

Everything was different now. I was no longer in Paris nor was I in my drafty old room at the orphanage. I was in my new home with Aunt Connie and Uncle Bates. It was a beautiful morning, and when I heard Love Bird's song I felt like singing, too:

Love Bird, Love Bird, I love you,
Mother Claudine, Father Lonnie,
Grandma, Grandpa,
and Clara Lee, too.

"*Bonjour, Aunt Connie and Uncle Bates. Bonjour, Lonnie,*" Love Bird said as he perched on my finger.

"Love Bird, we want to thank you for helping us find Lonnie," said Aunt Connie and Uncle Bates.

"And I want to thank you for helping me find my loved ones," I said. "You are real, Love Bird, and you are magic, too. You've changed my life with love. And I will never forget you, even though you are full of tricks."

"*Au revoir, Lonnie. Au revoir, Aunt Connie and Uncle Bates*. Till we meet again," said the beautiful Love Bird as he flew one last time through the window and was gone.

Mona Lisa: A painting by Leonardo da Vinci (born April 15, 1452, in Anchiano, Italy). At a time when most artists painted ornately attired women, da Vinci portrayed the plainly dressed, unadorned Lisa del Giocondo, who wears the most famous smile in history. The Mona Lisa hangs in the Louvre Museum in Paris.

Harlem Renaissance: Dating from 1919 to 1929, this period in American history was marked by a cultural, social, and political awakening among black Americans. The art, music, and writing of the period left a rich cultural legacy. The following figures lived and worked in New York City's Harlem district during this period:

Josephine Baker: Born on June 3, 1906, in Saint Louis, Missouri. She left Saint Louis at age thirteen to join a traveling show that toured Harlem. At eighteen she left Harlem and went to Paris to dance in La Revue Negre. Josephine Baker became one of France's most beloved singers and performers and acquired French citizenship in 1937. In 1973 she returned to New York to perform at Carnegie Hall and on the stage of the Apollo theater in Harlem.

Aaron Douglas: The best known painter of the Harlem Renaissance. He was born May 26, 1898, in Kansas. He painted a series of murals celebrating the spiritual and cultural elevation of African Americans. These murals are installed at Fisk University in Nashville, Tennessee, and the Harlem Branch of the New York Public Library.

Jesse Faust: Born April 26, 1882, in Camden, New Jersey. She was one of Cornell University's first black graduates, earning a B.A. degree there in 1905 and an M.A. from the University of Pennsylvania in 1919. She also studied at the Sorbonne in Paris and was the literary editor of the NAACP's (National Association for the Advancement of Colored People) *Crisis* magazine, which was known to support the cultural movement of the Harlem Renaissance. She was one of the best known poets, essayists, and novelists of the Harlem Renaissance.

Marcus Garvey and the Back to Africa Movement: Garvey was born in Saint Ann's Bay, Jamaica, on August 17, 1887. He came to Harlem in 1916 at age twenty-nine, whereupon he founded the Universal Negro Improvement Association that promoted racial self-respect. He started the *Negro World* newspaper in 1918 to carry his message. His Back to Africa Movement sold shares on his shipping line, the Black Star, which was intended to return African Americans to Africa.

Zora Neale Hurston: Born January 7, 1901, in Eatonville, Florida, an all-black town. She was the most prolific writer of the Harlem Renaissance period. Her many books—including *Mules and Men*; *Their Eyes Were Watching God*; *Moses, Man of the Mountain*; and her autobiography, *Dust Tracks on a Road*—continue to enjoy wide readership today.

Bibliography

Abella, Chana Byers. *The Children We Remember*. New York: Greenwood Books, 1983.

Borotolon, Llana. *The Life, Times, and Art of Leonardo*. Edited by Enzo Oriandi. Translated by C. J. Richards. Italy: Crown Press, 1965.

Keller, Bruce, ed. *The Harlem Renaissance: A Historical Dictionary for the Era*. Westport: Greenwood Press, 1984.

Kramer, Victor, ed. *The Harlem Renaissance Re-examined*. New York: Arns Press, 1987.

Maltin, Tony. *Marcus Garvey, Hero: A First Biography*. Dover: Majority Press, 1983.

Miers, Charles, ed. *Harlem Renaissance Art of Black America*. New York: Harry N. Abrams, Inc., 1987.

Prager, Arthur and Emily. *World War II Resistance Stories*. New York: Triumph Books, 1979.

Snyder, Louis L. *World War II*. New York: Franklin Watts, 1981.

Wiser, William. *The Great Good Place: American Expatriate Women in Paris*. New York: W. W. Norton and Company, 1991.

Faith Ringgold was born in Harlem in 1930. She now lives in Englewood, New Jersey. An artist of international renown, she began her artistic career more than 30 years ago as a painter. In the early 1970s she began to experiment with painting on unstretched canvases framed in cloth inspired by fourteenth-century Tibetan *tankas*—paintings on fabric that were framed with brightly colored silk brocades. These works are what Ms. Ringgold calls her "early quilts." Inspired by African art as well, she experimented with soft sculptural forms and masks, mixing the sewing she learned form her mother, Madame Willi Posey, who was a fashion designer and dressmaker, with traditional fine art forms she learned in school. Ms. Ringgold made her first quilt, "Echoes of Harlem," in 1980 as a collaboration with her mother.

Today, Faith Ringgold is best known for her painted story quilts—art that combines painting, quilted fabric, and storytelling. However, *Bonjour, Lonnie* was created as a children's book. Lonnie was first introduced as the adopted son of Aunt Connie and Uncle Bates in *Dinner at Aunt Connie's House*, published in 1993 and based on "The Dinner Quilt," which Ms. Ringgold created in 1986. It has been exhibited at major museums around the country and is now housed in a private collection.

Faith Ringgold is married to Burdette Ringgold and has two daughters and three granddaughters. She is a professor of art at the University of California, San Diego, in La Jolla, California, where she teaches for half the year. She has received more than 50 awards and honors for her art and books, including the Solomon R. Guggenheim Fellowship for painting and seven honorary doctorates, one of which is from the City College of New York, her alma mater.

Her first book, *Tar Beach*, was a Caldecott Honor Book and winner of the Coretta Scott King Award for illustration, among numerous other honors. *Bonjour, Lonnie* is Faith Ringgold's second book for Hyperion Books for Children.

I'd like to acknowledge the many people, both French and American, who helped me with this book. First, my then-assistant Vanessa P. Williams, who did the initial research, my daughter Barbara Wallace for the French passages, and the distinguished professor Michel Fabre of the Sorbonne, for his stories about the French resistance movement and the African American participation in the liberation of Paris; Professor Maica Sancone for her research on the Nazi occupation of Paris during World War II; my Paris friend, Mauricette Gilant; the French writer Nicole Bernheim; and my American friend, the art curator and writer Eleanor Flomenhaft— all of whom read the story and affirmed its relevance and supplied valuable input.

This book is dedicated to children of mixed racial parentage everywhere,
and to all the children orphaned by war and other forms of violence,
and to the many adoptive parents of these children
who love them as their own.

Printed in Hong Kong by South China Printing Company (1988) Ltd.

First Edition
1 3 5 7 9 10 8 6 4 2

The artwork for each picture is prepared using acrylic.
This book is set in 13-point Caxton.

Library of Congress Cataloging-in-Publication Data
Ringgold, Faith.
Bonjour, Lonnie / by Faith Ringgold.
p. cm.
Summary: An African-American Jewish boy traces his ancestry with
the help of the Love Bird of Paris.
ISBN 0-7868-0076-3 (trade)—ISBN 0-7868-2062-4 (lib. bdg.)
[1. Orphans—Fiction. 2. Birds—Fiction. 3. Paris (France)—
Fiction. 4. Afro-Americans—Fiction. 5. Jews—Fiction.
6. Family—Fiction.] I. Title.
PZ7.R4726Bo 1996
[Fic]—dc20 95-41146